Taking Care of
TROUBLE

Taking Care of TROUBLE

BONNIE GRAVES

illustrated by
Robin Preiss Glasser

Dutton Children's Books ✳ New York

Text copyright © 2002 by Bonnie Graves
Illustrations copyright © 2002 by Robin Preiss Glasser

CIP Data is available.

Published in the United States by Dutton Children's Books,
a division of Penguin Putnam Books for Young Readers
345 Hudson Street, New York, New York 10014
www.penguinputnam.com

Designed by Alyssa Morris
Printed in USA • First Edition
ISBN 0-525-46830-7
1 3 5 7 9 10 8 6 4 2

*For Julie and Erin—the brilliant, no-trouble
daughters who inspired this story—with love*

—B.G.

For Aaron and Kevin, with love

—R.P.G.

With special thanks to Meredith Mundy Wasinger,
the brilliant, no-trouble editor who
brought this book to life

Contents

Taking Care of
TROUBLE

1
Emergency!

Joel Maccarone sat in his backyard reading his Emergency Preparedness manual. He had reached page 25. Yuck! There it was—spurting blood wounds, that gross picture that always horrified him. He forced himself to keep his eyes open and read. At that very same moment he heard a shriek from the other side of the hedge. It came from a girl—one he knew.

"No! I can't believe it! I'm going to die!" cried the voice.

Joel's heart started pumping overtime. He jumped up and peered over the hedge. Rachel Rottenberger stood at the edge of the neighbor's patio, holding a cordless phone up to her ear. Tucker Goodchild squatted in the sandbox, throwing sand at her bare legs. Rachel was the Goodchilds' babysitter and Joel's best friend Ralphie's sister.

"Oh, this is awful. I can't believe it!" she went on, twisting one of her million curls around her finger.

And then Rachel saw him. Their eyes met, eyeball-to-eyeball. Joel ducked out of sight. But not soon enough.

"Joel!" she called.

Joel's skin prickled—it always did when he panicked. He felt like he was being stung by an army of red ants or poked with a million needles.

"Joel!" Rachel said again.

Help! Why was she calling *him?* He didn't need a real emergency right now. The next Emergency Preparedness drill was tomorrow. It was the last

one before the Junior Adventurers' mountain-biking trip to the Rockies. He had to pass it this time, or he couldn't go. He flopped back down on the grass and buried his face in his book. The words *Keep calm. Don't panic* leaped out at him.

Before he knew it, she was standing over him. Tucker rode on Rachel's hip. He wore striped overalls and no shirt, his legs wrapped around Rachel's cutoff jeans shorts.

Tucker pulled a handful of leaves off the hedge and threw them at Joel.

"You've got to help me out, Joel," Rachel said.

Joel. Why did she keep saying his name? He didn't think she even *knew* his name, although he had been at her house—Ralphie's house—about a kajillion times. "I've got an emergency," she said.

"Emergency?" The word stuck in his throat and made his skin prickle again. He was the only kid in Junior Adventurers who had flunked EP twice. Rachel had to know this. It was public knowledge.

Besides, Rachel's dad was their JA leader. He could picture the Rottenbergers sitting around the dinner table cracking up over the last EP drill. During that one, Joel had gotten so flustered he mistook the mess kit for the first-aid kit and dialed 991 instead of 911.

"Yes, emergency," Rachel repeated, breathlessly. "Amanda just called. Scum and the Suds are playing at the mall. At noon. I've *got* to see them! I'll just die if I don't!"

That was an emergency, all right. But what was he supposed to do?

"Please watch Tucker for me," she said.

"Watch Tucker?" Joel sputtered. Watch the kid Rachel had nicknamed *Trouble*? Yikes! A fate *worse* than death.

Something too horrible to think about would happen while Rachel and Amanda were going maniac over Scum and the Suds! Joel imagined broken bones jutting out of skin or—even scarier—

spurting blood wounds. He felt a little dizzy and made the mistake of glancing down at the cover of the EP manual. It pictured a bandaged victim being hauled off on a stretcher.

"It'll only be for an hour or so. Please!"

I'm only eleven! he wanted to yell. *Practically a kid myself.* Instead he said, "Rachel, I, ah . . . "

"Oh, come on, Joel. Ralphie told me you were the smartest kid in fifth grade. Besides, I know you just earned your JA baby-sitting badge. Watching Tucker will be a piece of cake."

Yeah, devil's food cake.

"Look at Tucker. He's an angel," Rachel cooed.

Joel glanced at Tucker. His chubby cheeks looked like two ripe peaches and his big brown eyes stared right into Joel's. Then Tucker spit out a mouthful of chewed-up leaves mixed with slobber.

"Doe!" Tucker said, his arm snapping out in front of him like the blade on a jackknife.

"See, he even knows your name!"

Help! Joel's arms prickled so much he had to scratch. How could he turn Rachel down? But how could he watch Tucker? Impossible.

And then in a flash, the perfect alibi came to him. "Gee, Rachel, I'd like to help you out, but . . . ah, I can't. My mom's working today. She calls every hour on the hour. If I'm not here, she'll wig out."

"Simple. Call her. Say you're at the Goodchilds'. Tell her it's an emergency."

"Wow. Why hadn't I thought of that? That's a *great* idea," Joel said, smiling for the first time. Rachel had just solved the whole problem. An emergency. Ha! His mother would never let him baby-sit Tucker, then. Not in a million years. Not until he had passed EP, anyway. And that wasn't until tomorrow.

2
"You're scared, aren't you?"

ere. Use this," Rachel said, handing him the cordless phone.

Joel punched in the phone number at Pets Are Pals.

Rachel set Tucker down, and he bolted after a squirrel through a break in the hedge that separated the two yards. Rachel chased after him.

Joel listened to the phone ring five times. He was about to hang up when he heard his mom's recorded voice. "Pets Are Pals. We're with a guest right now, but if you leave your name and number, we'll return your call. Thank you."

Click. He hung up.

"Did you tell her?" Rachel called from the Goodchilds' backyard. She scooped up Tucker. He screamed and beat his fists against Rachel's chest.

"I got the answering machine," Joel said as he walked into the Goodchilds' yard to return the phone.

"Did you leave a message?" Now she stood in front of him. She set Tucker back in the sandbox. Tucker crawled away.

"Message?"

"That you were baby-sitting at the Goodchilds'?"

Joel shook his head. "She'd kill me. I have to talk to her. Voice-to-voice, I mean."

Rachel looked over Joel's shoulder. She gasped. "Tucker! No!"

Joel turned around. There sat Tucker licking dirt off a rock. Suddenly the rock disappeared into his mouth.

Like a streak of lightning, Rachel bolted toward Tucker. She plunged her finger into his mouth. Out popped the rock. "Rocks are yucky," she told Tucker, picking him up. "Here." She pulled a pacifier out of her pocket and stuck it into Tucker's mouth.

Rachel walked back toward Joel, smiling as if she was about to hand him a ticket to Adventure World. Tucker's right hand, Joel noticed, was curled into a tight fist. What had Trouble managed to snatch this time?

"Joel, please watch Tucker. Puh-*lease*?" Even holding Tucker, Rachel managed to put both her palms together as if she were praying. If it hadn't been for Tucker, she probably would have gotten down on her knees, too. Rachel, who hardly ever

spoke to him, was now begging, *pleading* with him. "This is an *emergency*!"

Joel was pretty sure his mom wouldn't think a Scum and the Suds concert was an emergency. He glanced over at Tucker. And Joel was absolutely sure his mom would skin him alive if he did this without asking. "I know, Rachel. But . . . I mean . . . it's just that . . . "

She stared at him. "I know! You're scared, aren't you? Because you haven't passed EP, I mean."

Did she have to rub it in?

"Listen, Joel. Nothing's going to happen. Tucker's a really good kid, honest. Nothing you can't handle."

Tucker smiled, opened his fist, and hurled his stash of rocks in Joel's direction. *Clunk. Clunk. Clunk.* They landed at Joel's feet. Rachel lifted Tucker back into the sandbox.

"Listen, Amanda says they're giving out T-shirts to the hundred kids who scream the loudest. If you'll watch Tucker, I promise I'll yell so loud, you'll be able to hear me from the mall. That Scum and the Suds T-shirt will be yours. Just say you'll watch Tucker. Please, please, please!"

Joel had never before seen Rachel look like this. Her face reminded him of one of the earthquake victims he'd seen on the Emergency Preparedness video, a little girl in the rubble waiting for someone to rescue her. Turning Rachel down would be like turning his back on that homeless girl. He could never be so heartless. Besides, a Scum and the Suds T-shirt? How could he pass up *that?*

"OK," he said. As soon as the word slipped out, he wanted to take it back, but Rachel already had Amanda on the line. Tucker, again out of the sandbox, stood directly in front of him and let loose another rock. It hit Joel in the chest, right between the words *Junior* and *Adventurer* on his T-shirt.

"He's going to do it!" Rachel screamed into the phone. She smiled and looked at Joel. "Amanda says you're totally awesome."

This was too much. A few minutes earlier, Rachel didn't even know he existed. And now she was going to ruin her vocal cords just to get him a T-shirt, and Amanda, the most popular girl at Arthur B. Stone Middle School, was calling him awesome. The sun beat down on his head. Tucker clomped on Joel's bare foot with his Gerber hightops. Joel felt dizzy.

Rachel handed him the phone. "Call your mom quick and leave a message. Then I'll show you what to do. But we've got to hurry!"

Joel wiped the sweat out of his eyes and tried Pets Are Pals again. He cleared the huge lump out of his throat. After the beep, he said, "Hi, Mom. It's me, Joel. An emergency at the Goodchilds'. I'm babysitting Tucker. Bye." His head throbbed and his skin prickled worse than ever. What had he gotten himself into?

3
Help! Help!

Rachel slid the patio door open, and Joel followed her inside.

Tucker clung to Rachel like tooth plaque, his legs wrapped around her waist, arms around her neck. Tucker must have suspected something was up. Like he knew his life was going to be in the hands of a total loser.

On the way to the kitchen, Rachel asked, "Have you ever met Captain?"

Joel tripped over something. After being in the sun so long, his eyes hadn't adjusted to the darkness. Captain? Who the heck was Captain? Had the Goodchilds gotten a dog? A huge hairy one that slobbered? Or maybe Captain was a relative? A bald uncle with a peg leg and a gold tooth?

In the kitchen, Rachel pointed to a cage. "There he is!"

Captain whistled and cocked his head.

"He's a cockatoo. I guess he says a few things, but I haven't heard them yet." Rachel leaned close to the cage. "Pretty boy," she said.

Captain whistled.

Joel felt relieved. A bird he could handle. Especially one in a cage, one that looked as harmless as Captain. The bird was about the size of a blue jay and had small dark beady eyes, a tuft of gray feathers that sat up on his head like a Burger King crown, and a round dab of rouge on each cheek. "Princess" would have been a better name.

Tucker pounded his hand on the cage. "Boy," he said.

"Bird," Rachel corrected. "Tucker doesn't say much. Kind of like you, Joel. But once in a while he'll surprise you. I think he's really smart and just doesn't want to let on." She winked at Joel. Man. He hoped his face wasn't as red as it felt!

Rachel picked up a tablet of paper from the table. "Here's Tucker's schedule. Mrs. G will be home at four, and I'll be back by two *at the latest*. Oh, and I'd better warn you. You may have a visitor. Mrs. Rainershine from down the street. She comes by every afternoon . . . to *give* the Goodchilds something. Yesterday she gave me this blank tape. She said it was a story without words. Can you believe it? Like I was actually going to put it in my Walkman and listen to a lot of silence? Major weirdness."

Rachel pointed at her temple and drew circles with her finger.

Yeah. He knew about Mrs. Rainershine, the neighbor his dad said was a couple of cards shy of a full deck. Ralphie used to call her up and ask her dumb stuff like, "Is your refrigerator running?" And then say, "Well, it just ran past the window. You'd better catch it."

"Here's Mrs. G's number. But please, Joel. She *can't* know I left Tucker. Only call her if it's an absolute emergency."

"Emergency?" Joel muttered. The dreaded *E* word, and the only word he'd uttered since "OK." He scratched both his arms violently.

"Life or death only," she said. "But don't worry. I know you and Tucker will do great." Rachel pried Tucker's arms and legs loose and handed him to Joel, wriggling and kicking.

Help! No way could he handle this kid alone. As soon as Rachel left he would call Ralphie.

"Oh, and one more thing, Joel. *Don't* let Ralphie in. He's a walking emergency himself!" She turned and ran out of the house.

"Opah! Opah!" Tucker shrieked.

Help! Help! Joel cried inside.

4
"Man Overboard!"

Over Tucker's howls, Joel heard a pounding on the door. The police! He was sure of it. Someone had reported Tucker's screams, and the police were coming to arrest him.

"What's happening in there?" He knew the voice.

The door burst open and in barged Ralphie, a camcorder mounted on his shoulder. He started shooting, the camcorder aimed right at Joel.

Joel stared at him, stunned. "How'd you know I was here? And what are you *doing?*"

"Rachel told me when she came home to get her bike. Thought I'd get some footage for the *World's Funniest Videos*," Ralphie announced, one eye squeezed shut and the other peering into the camera lens. Ever since Ralphie's uncle had given him his old camcorder, Ralphie had been trying to cut footage for the *Funniest Videos*. "Hey, what's happening? What's Trouble doing now?" Ralphie asked, his eye still glued to the lens.

Tucker had stopped crying and was staring into the camera.

"Rachel told me not to let you in," Joel said.

"Yeah. She warned me to stay away, too." Ralphie took the camcorder from his eye. "But how could I stay away when my best friend, and the only JA who hasn't passed EP, volunteered to baby-sit Trouble? I'm here to help, man."

"I thought you were shooting for *Funniest Videos*," Joel said.

"That, too."

"I don't know, Rottenberger," Joel said, looking nervously at Tucker, who gaped openmouthed at Ralphie.

"You *know* there's going to be an emergency," Ralphie said. "Two heads are better than one. Especially when one of the heads is yours." Ralphie slapped his thigh and laughed. "If you get what I mean."

Joel thought it over. He and Ralphie had been friends since kindergarten. Macaroni and Rotten Burger, the kids called them. A couple of cafeteria items. Ralphie was round and plump, like a burger. Joel was tall and skinny, more like spaghetti than macaroni, really.

"OK. But no funny stuff. I mean it. This isn't like a practice drill. This is the real thing. I can't blow this one."

Ralphie stared at his friend. Now Tucker was looking at him, too. "You're right. Listen. I've got a great idea. I'll get it on tape. Record how you handle an emergency. Then I'll give my dad the tape so you won't have to go through that stupid EP drill tomorrow!" Ralphie smiled at Joel. "What d'you say? Brilliant, no?"

Joel considered the idea. What if he flunked again? That meant no Colorado and no mountain biking. His mom had said he could help her at Pets Are Pals while his friends were gone. But what was shampooing dogs and clipping cat claws when he could be cruising down a mountain?

Suddenly, Tucker bellowed again, mouth wide, eyes squeezed shut, face hot-sauce red.

Joel tried jiggling Tucker, a method he'd seen his Aunt Betty use with his little cousin Sarah. "Shh, shh. It's all right."

Ralphie started recording.

"Turn it off, Rottenberger. Nothing funny here. And no emergency," Joel said.

"Looks like you've got one to me," Ralphie yelled over Tucker's yowls. "And, like I said, I'm here to help. For starters, I'll show you how to keep Tucker quiet. But I'll record it like it was your idea. Follow me."

Joel, carrying the wailing Tucker, followed Ralphie into the kitchen.

Ralphie pulled a brown-and-white container of mocha fudge out of the freezer.

Tucker took in a couple of quivering breaths, then stopped and gazed at the ice cream.

Silence. How wonderful it sounded. Like Mrs. Rainershine's story-without-words.

"Ice cream. The miracure," Ralphie said, grinning like a talk-show host. "Rachel told me." He pointed to a high chair in front of Captain's cage. "Put him in there. And I'll start recording."

"The chair?"

"Well, what else, Maccarone? The birdcage?"

Joel studied the chair. So how *did* you get a baby into a high chair? He stared at the space between the chair back and the tray. Joel lifted Tucker up over the high chair and tried threading him between the chair back and the tray. Tucker wouldn't bend his legs. Instead, he stood on the chair seat, stiff as a soldier. His eyes were wide, his mouth open, drool oozing from the corner.

"Sit down, Tucker, and you can have some ice cream," Joel said as coaxingly as he could. He could hear the camcorder humming.

Tucker tried moving his rump down, but it wasn't the right motion. His body folded in half. Rump wedged in the seat. Feet flailing the air.

Ralphie howled with laughter and kept recording.

"Stop the camera!" Joel yelled. "You said you were here to help, Rottenberger!"

"OK, OK. Take the tray off, Maccarone. Squeeze those metal things on the sides. Then it'll slide off. I'll start recording again."

Joel squeezed on the metal bars and yanked the tray off. All the way off. He fell back on the floor

and Tucker bounced out of the chair, right on top of Joel. Tucker started wailing.

"Man overboard!" Captain squawked. *So that's why they call him Captain*, Joel thought.

"Don't cry, buddy," Joel told Tucker. "You're OK. Let's get you some ice cream."

"Opah! Opah!" Tucker cried.

Joel scooped Tucker up, set him in the chair, and slid the tray back on. Then he took the bowl of ice cream that Ralphie had dished up and gave it to Tucker.

Immediately, he dug into the pale brown mound. Spoon to mouth. Spoon to cheek.

Ralphie zoomed in with the camcorder.

Spoon to mouth. Mouth to bowl.

Joel watched in a trance as Tucker's face became a mask of chocolate.

The camcorder hummed.

"Hey, this is great!" Ralphie said. "Way to go, Tucker. You want to be on TV, don't you? A star!"

"P.U.," Captain shrieked, and ruffled his feathers.

Joel ran to the sink to get a washrag for Tucker's face.

Ralphie moved in for a close-up.

"Move!" Joel yelled at Ralphie as he tried to reach Tucker with the wet washrag. He shoved Ralphie. Ralphie lost his balance and fell against the high chair. It toppled over onto the birdcage. The ice cream sailed across the room. And so did Captain.

"Opah! Opah!" Tucker howled, still in the chair.

"Man overboard!" Captain called from his perch on the coatrack.

Just then, the telephone rang.

5
Oprah to the Rescue

First he had to get Tucker out of the chair.

"It's OK, buddy," he said to Tucker, kneeling beside him on the floor. He pulled the tray off and lifted out the sobbing Tucker. Tucker's arms reached up for Joel. His hands felt warm and sticky on the back of Joel's neck, his legs like a boa constrictor around Joel's waist.

"Man overboard!" Captain squawked again.

The phone rang for the fourth time.

What if it was Mrs. Goodchild? What would

he tell her? That Rachel had abandoned ship? He *couldn't.*

The phone rang for the fifth time. Maybe he just wouldn't answer it. But what if it was something really important?

The phone didn't ring again. Instead, a voice said, "Hello. You have reached the Goodchilds'. We can't come to the phone right now. Please leave your name and number, and we'll get back to you as soon as we can. Thank you."

"Joel! This is your mother. Call me back immediately!" He heard dogs barking in the background.

Still holding Tucker, Joel punched in the Pets Are Pals number. "Hi, Mom."

"Joel, what's going on?" He could hardly hear her over Tucker's sobs.

"Mom, I can't talk now."

"I can hear that, Joel. Why are you at the Goodchilds'? What was the emergency? Is everything OK?" *Woof. Woof.*

"Everything's fine. I'll explain later."

Captain flapped his wings and made a beeline for Joel's head.

Ralphie started recording.

Joel waved at him to stop, but Ralphie ignored him.

"Are you sure? What's wrong with Tucker?" his mom asked.

"Nothing, Mom. He just wants some ice cream." Captain started pecking on Joel's scalp.

"Ice cream? Where's Rachel?"

"Like I said. She had an emergency, Mom."

"What sort of emergency? Are you sure you don't need some help? I could leave the shop. I could be there in half an hour."

"No, Mom. I'll take care of this. Tucker's fine."

"P.U.!" Captain shrieked.

"What was that?"

"Nothing. I've got to go, Mom. Bye." *Click.* Joel hung up. "Put down that camcorder!" Joel shouted.

"Opah, opah," Tucker whimpered, and stuck his fingers in his mouth.

Joel turned his face toward Tucker's. "What's *opah?*" Joel asked Tucker.

"Opah," Tucker whimpered.

Joel turned toward Ralphie. "Turn that thing *off!*"

Ralphie took the camera away from his eye.

"All right, Rottenberger," Joel said, still jiggling Tucker up and down. "Since you're so smart, what's Tucker saying? What does *opah* mean?"

"Opah, opah." Tucker sniffed.

"Oprah. That's what he's saying. You know that talk show? My sister loves it. She's probably got Tucker hooked on it, too."

"OK, Tucker. We'll see if Oprah's on. First, let's get you cleaned up a little." Joel took a rag to Tucker's face, gently rubbing the dried ice cream off his chubby cheeks. "You want to watch Oprah?"

"Opah," Tucker said.

"P.U.," whistled Captain, and flew through the doorway into the living room.

"OK. Let's go."

As Joel finished wiping Tucker's sticky hands with the wet rag, his eyes caught the mess in the kitchen—streaks of ice cream had dried on the wallpaper and cabinets. Tucker's dish lay upside down in a brown puddle near the middle of the kitchen floor. Next to the fallen high chair lay Captain's capsized cage. Well, he would take care of everything later. He still had plenty of time before Rachel got back. Lots of time. He'd been here only a few minutes and already it seemed like several lifetimes.

He carried Tucker into the living room. Maybe if he really got lucky, Oprah would have Dr. Dribbel, the baby doctor, on the show today. He'd seen him on another show. Moms called in with all sorts of baby problems. Dr. Dribbel could answer every single one of them.

Ralphie had his arm stretched out in front of him, aiming the remote at the TV. "Darn thing doesn't work."

"Let me try. Maybe you're not close enough." Joel moved closer to the TV with the remote, but still nothing.

Joel set Tucker on the floor. His arm had gotten so stiff from holding him, it felt numb. "Sit here, Tucker."

Quickly Joel pressed the on/off control on the TV. An image appeared on the screen. It wasn't Oprah or even Dr. Dribbel, but Big Bird. As Big Bird sang and danced, Joel smiled. Funny how he could instantly remember exactly how it felt to be five again. Happy. That's how it felt. No EP drills. No troubles. Just sunny days and other people taking care of you.

"Flip channels, Maccarone. I think Oprah's on now," Ralphie said.

Joel pressed the channel changer and watched the screen as he scanned through the channels.

"Stop!" Ralphie yelled. "There she is!"

Joel turned around to tell Tucker. "Here's Oprah!"

But Tucker was gone.

6
"Call 911!"

Tucker!" Joel shouted, then spotted Tucker's pudgy bottom sticking out from under the coffee table. "Tucker, what are you doing under there?" Joel asked, relieved that Tucker had crawled only to the coffee table and not to the basement steps. He could already hear Courtney Chang on the evening news: "Toddler tumbles to his death while baby-sitter watches Oprah." His skin prickled. He carefully grabbed Tucker by the waist and scooted him out from under the table.

When he turned Tucker around and saw his face, horror shot through him. "Oh, no!" he gasped. "This can't be happening!"

"Yikes!" yelled Ralphie. "Call 911!"

Blood covered Tucker's lips. It ran out of his mouth, trickling over his chin and onto his overalls. He looked like a baby vampire.

Joel's heart forgot to pump. He couldn't move. What had Tucker done?

"Call 911!" Ralphie screamed again.

The phone! With Tucker in his arms, Joel ran to the kitchen. Where had he put the phone? He didn't see it anywhere.

Then the chair seat began ringing. The phone must have dropped from the table and landed on the chair!

Captain shot by, whistled, and perched on the chair back.

As Joel picked up the phone, a red glob fell out of Tucker's mouth and onto the floor. Joel couldn't believe his eyes. It was a slimy red chalk-crayon. No wonder it looked like blood. He and Ralphie had used the same stuff last Halloween on their Dracula costumes. Thank goodness it wasn't Tucker's tongue.

"Nice job, matey!" Captain squawked.

The phone rang again. Without thinking, he answered it.

"Goodchilds'," Joel panted into the phone.

"Maybe Tucker's wet," his mom said. A cat meowed.

"Mom!" Joel shouted.

"It's very important to keep babies dry. You don't want Tucker to get diaper rash."

Man. If his mom could see Tucker's face, she wouldn't be worrying about a little thing like diaper rash.

"Rachel can be scatterbrained sometimes," Joel's mom continued. *Meow*. "I can see her forgetting something important like diapers. What happened to Rachel anyway? Where is she?"

Joel scanned the kitchen for diapers. Come to think of it, Rachel *hadn't* said anything about diapers.

"Mom. I'll find the diapers. I'll change Tucker if he's wet. Now don't worry. Good-bye." *Click.*

Man, oh, man. Why did his mother treat him like *he* was the baby?

"Put that camera down, Rottenberger, and help me look for diapers!"

"Diapers?"

Joel reached up to scratch his head, and Captain started pecking it. "Ow! Get off!"

"Man overboard!" Captain shrieked from the chandelier.

Joel reached into Tucker's overalls to feel his diapers. The cotton diaper was sopping wet. And the smell. Yuck. It was so strong it stung the inside of

Joel's nose and made his eyes water. He *had* to find those diapers.

Tucker whimpered and slurped on his fingers. "Opah."

"We'll watch Oprah later. First we'll change you. Then you'll feel better."

Ralphie slapped his thigh and laughed. "Man. I've got to see this one. Better yet, I'll get it on tape."

"Forget it, Rottenberger. This is serious. Now help me."

Joel wet the rag again and cleaned up Tucker's face. The kitchen wall and cabinets were still a mess, the floor grosser than ever. Later. He would take care of that later. First things first. Floors, cabinets, and walls didn't smell nasty or get rashes. He had to find those diapers—and fast.

Carrying Tucker on his hip, Joel searched every room in the house. Nothing. Not a diaper in sight. He even checked the drawers in Tucker's room. Now he could feel the wet coming through Tucker's overalls. This was getting serious. He had to figure something out. He had to. *Use your brain. Use the resources at hand*. Wasn't that what the EP manual said? Well, he had a brain. But what resources? What could he use for a diaper? And then like a bolt of lightning, or a miracle from heaven, the solution flashed in his brain. He knew exactly what he would do.

"OK, Rottenberger. If you've got to record, get this."

Joel checked the kitchen drawers until he found a plastic bag. Then he carried Tucker to the living room and laid him on the carpet. Tucker looked up at Joel as if he knew exactly what Joel was going to do.

Joel unhooked Tucker's wet overalls and pulled them off. Then the plastic pants. Next he unpinned the diapers. There wasn't a dry spot left. Thank goodness, no rash, though. Joel held his breath. He pinched a corner of the diaper with his finger and thumb and dropped it into the plastic bag. *Zip.* There. Locked tight. Smell and all.

A little squeal escaped from Tucker. "Ah-bah," he said.

Joel grabbed the bottom of his Junior Adventurer T-shirt and yanked it off.

"Maccarone? What are you doing?" Ralphie asked. The camcorder whirred.

"Just watch!" Joel folded his T-shirt into a neat rectangle. Next he took both Tucker's ankles in one hand and raised Tucker's bottom up. Then he slid his folded Junior Adventurer T-shirt underneath. He brought the front and back of one side of the rectangle together and pinned it and then did the other side. He lifted Tucker to a standing position. Immediately the T-shirt diaper slid to the floor.

"Turn that thing off!" Joel yelled at Ralphie. He couldn't let Ralphie tape Tucker naked! What if Ralphie's video really did get on TV?

Joel lifted the T-shirt diaper off the floor and up

over Tucker's bottom once again. He found Tucker's plastic pants on the floor and pulled them over the makeshift diaper. That should do it. "There you go, Tucker. All set. Nice and dry."

Tucker scrunched up his face. His ripe-peach cheeks turned apple red. He made strange grunting sounds.

"He's doing it!" Ralphie shouted.

"Doing what?"

"Number two! He's pooping in your T-shirt!"

7
More Trouble

Ralphie laughed like a lunatic and pointed his finger at Tucker. "Now you know why my sister calls him Trouble!"

Tucker's bottom lip stuck out, and his chin began to tremble.

"Shut up, Rottenberger. Now look what you've done. It's not Tucker's fault."

"But your shirt, Maccarone! He's ruined your JA shirt!" Ralphie pinched his nostrils together. "P.U. Gross!"

"P.U.," Captain echoed from his perch on the lamp.

"Opah, opah!" Tucker sobbed.

"So what are you going to do now, Maccarone?"

Yeah. What *was* he going to do? Call Mrs. Goodchild? But what about Rachel? She would lose her summer baby-sitting job. All on account of him.

"Ralphie, you've got to go buy some diapers."

"With what?" Ralphie asked, still pinching his nose.

"You don't have any money?"

"No. Do you?"

Joel fished in his pockets, but he knew all he'd find was lint.

Then Joel heard a woman's voice outside. His heart lurched.

He shot a look at Ralphie.

Ralphie shrugged. "Maybe it's Mrs. G," he whispered. "Look. There's her laptop computer on the table. She's probably come to get it!"

"Oh, man. It can't be." Every inch of Joel's skin prickled. The hairs on his arms stood at attention. He shivered, suddenly realizing he was half naked. "She can't see the place like this! And look at Tucker!"

Tucker's plastic pants hung down to his dimpled knees. By now he probably had an advanced case of diaper rash. His lips were still blood red from the chalk, and his hair stuck up in spikes where he had run his chocolatey fingers through it. And what would Mrs. Goodchild think about the disaster in the kitchen? And Captain flying all over the house? He knew he was going to get killed. The only question was by whom—Mrs. G, his mom, or Rachel? Or all three? Was there such a thing as a triple murder of the same person?

Joel heard the voice again, somewhere outside, near the kitchen bay window. Yikes! What was he going to do? He grabbed Tucker and ran to the window. Mrs. Rainershine! She was singing. Joel couldn't tell if she was singing to herself or sere-nading the Goodchilds' shrubbery.

Soon there was a rapping at the kitchen door.

Joel opened the door. What else could he do?

And there stood Mrs. Rainershine, holding an empty quart jar. She gazed at him through a pair of lenses so thick that her eyes looked like two shriv-eled peas. "Rachel! You got your hair cut, dear," she said. And then she zeroed in on Joel's bare chest. "Oh, my!"

Ralphie bent over and howled with laughter.

"It's me, Joel Maccarone. I'm watching Tucker today."

At that moment, Captain flew up behind Joel and lit on his shoulder. Captain's talons dug into his bare skin. "OUCH!"

Oh no! The door was wide open! The great out-doors spread before Captain like a wide-screen TV.

"Man overboard!" Captain squawked.

8
Fresh Air

Joel grabbed the doorknob and slammed the door on Mrs. Rainershine. He had no choice.

Captain flapped his wings and took off out of the kitchen.

Joel opened the door again, just wide enough to see Mrs. Rainershine. She wore a floppy straw hat, a red dress covered with flowers in every shade of the rainbow, and hiking boots. She stared at him through her thick spectacles, her eyes as small and round as Captain's.

"Sorry," Joel said. "The Goodchilds' cockatoo's on the loose, and I thought he'd escape."

Mrs. Rainershine's mouth curled up at the corners and opened. "Oh," she said. "I've come to give you something." She started walking into the kitchen.

Yikes! What would she do when she saw the mess?

"I hope you can use this. I found a jar of it when I was cleaning my cupboards. I'd almost forgot I'd trapped a quart when Mr. Rainershine and I were hiking in the Rockies." She held up the empty quart jar. "Pure mountain air," she said. "Some people go to the mountains for big game, birds, or fish. Me? I go for fresh air." As she stepped in, Joel reached for the doorknob and closed the door behind her.

Ralphie was laughing so hard, Joel was sure he would wet his pants.

Mrs. Rainershine set the jar of fresh air on the counter and looked around the kitchen. The sun streamed through the windows, spotlighting each disaster—the cage with all its droppings, the dried ice cream on the wall, cabinets, and floor, the toppled high chair. "Lovely room," said Mrs. Rainershine.

Joel stared at Mrs. Rainershine. She smiled.

Ralphie kept shooting away with his camcorder, but Mrs. Rainershine didn't say a word. Didn't she see him? Didn't she see *anything?*

"And how are you, my sweet Tucker?" she said, placing her hand under his chin. Tucker turned away and pressed his face against Joel's neck. "Ah, my. What a happy child. I can see you are a wonderful baby-sitter, Joel."

"P.U.," Captain said.

"Loony-tunes," said Ralphie, under his breath.

"Well, sorry I must leave so soon. But I must

be on my way," said Mrs. Rainershine. "There's no time like the present! Enjoy the fresh air." She opened the door and disappeared outside.

Joel scowled at Ralphie. "That was really lame, Rottenberger."

"What?"

"Saying, 'Loony-tunes' and laughing out loud. Not to mention sticking that stupid camcorder in her face."

"Geez, Maccarone. She couldn't see me anyway. And how could you take her jar of stupid fresh air and not crack up yourself? Not that it isn't just what this place needs anyway, fresh air. P.U."

"P.U.," echoed Captain.

"How can you stand it?" Ralphie grabbed his throat and made gagging sounds.

"Well, why don't you just leave, then?"

Ralphie stared at Joel. "What?"

"I said why don't you leave? No one invited you anyway."

"But . . . what about the EP tape?" Ralphie asked.

"Forget it. I'll just do the drill tomorrow like everyone else."

"Big mistake, Maccarone. But go ahead. Flunk the EP drill. See if I care. I got other uses for this tape." Ralphie patted the camcorder. "I'm outta here."

And he was, camcorder and all.

So what? Rachel was right. Ralphie had only caused trouble.

"Good riddance," he told Tucker. He'd been carrying the kid around for so long he felt like they were attached.

After Ralphie left, Joel took a good look at the mess in the kitchen. Rachel would never give him the Scum and the Suds T-shirt if she saw the place like this. Where should he start? *Keep calm. Don't panic.* He took a deep breath. Yuck. He had to get Tucker out of that diaper. Joel spotted Mrs. Rainershine's quart jar sitting on the counter. He smiled.

What the heck? He unscrewed the top and let the fresh air escape into the room.

"OK, Tucker. It's just you and me, buddy. And we're going to do it."

First Joel righted the high chair and then the birdcage. He got a broom and with one hand swept the sand, mixed with Captain's droppings, out the door. Next he picked up the ice-cream bowl, set it in the sink, and turned the water on. Tucker giggled as he rode on Joel's hip around the kitchen.

"Good boy," Joel said, tapping the tip of Tucker's nose. "This is fun, huh?" Joel couldn't even smell the diaper anymore.

Joel pulled a wad of paper towels from the holder, wet them, and cleaned up the ice-cream mess on the wall, cabinets, and the floor.

The phone rang.

"Hello, Goodchilds'."

"Did you change Tucker?" his mom asked. *Meow. Woof.*

"Yes, Mom. I changed Tucker. Now good-bye!"

He looked at Tucker. "Here's the deal about moms," he confided. "They think you're a baby even when you're not. But you heard Mrs. Rainershine. She said I was a wonderful baby-sitter. And then there's Rachel. She trusts me, too. She's bringing me a Scum and the Suds T-shirt. Now we'll clean *you* up, buddy. Let's go!"

9
Scum and the Suds

In the bathroom, Joel ran water in the tub. Then he set Tucker on the floor. The time had finally come. He had to do it. Take off that diaper. He swallowed hard, unpinned the T-shirt diaper, and slid it off Tucker. Tucker smiled at Joel, but the smell was so gross, Joel couldn't help making a face. Tucker saw him, and his smile disappeared. Joel wanted to hold his nose and shut his eyes, but he didn't. He kept them wide open and breathed through his mouth. It wasn't Tucker's fault. Babies messed their pants. That was just part of being a baby.

"That's a big boy, Tucker. You stand nice and still." Tucker stood quietly and kept staring at Joel.

So he had the T-shirt off. Now what? What did he do next? What should he do with the T-shirt? He looked at the wastebasket. He couldn't throw it in there. Yuck. Sicko. He set it on the tile floor next to the toilet.

Joel tested the water in the tub with his elbow, a technique he'd learned getting his JA baby-sitting badge. The temperature seemed just right, so he lifted Tucker into the tub. Tucker squealed, sat down, and began patting the water. Joel launched Tucker's rubber ducky and boats from the side of the tub. Then he took a washcloth in his hand.

"Look, Tucker. See this? I'm going to get it wet and sudsy. Then I'm going to wash you all over so you look like a million bucks when Rachel gets home. How 'bout that?"

Joel couldn't tell how Tucker felt about this idea. He was too busy pushing his boats through the water.

Joel made his move with the cloth—hair, face, arms. When Tucker leaned forward to grab his duck that had drifted out of reach, Joel quickly washed his bottom. He'd done it! Washed the whole of Tucker.

But still, there it sat—the JA T-shirt he'd used for a diaper—next to the toilet. The toilet! That was it! He could just *flush* the whole mess.

Keeping a careful eye on Tucker in the tub, Joel picked up the soiled T-shirt, emptied its contents into the toilet, and flushed. He stared at his favorite shirt. How lame. Of course he couldn't flush *it!* He took the dripping shirt, opened the bathroom window, and dropped it outside. He would pick it up later.

Joel glanced at his watch. One-thirty. "Well, Tucker, old buddy. You may have to stay in the tub till Rachel gets home. I just can't find your diapers. Too bad *you* can't tell me where they are."

"Coset," Tucker said.

Joel's mouth fell open. "What did you say?"

Tucker pointed to a small closet within arm's reach of the tub. "Coset," he said again.

Joel opened the closet door. There sat a box of disposable diapers—the pull-up kind. He grabbed one and showed it to Tucker. "You're a genius, Tucker. Smartest baby alive. Know that?"

Tucker smiled and slapped the water. He kept at it until his boats rocked violently on Tucker's stormy sea.

"Hey! You're getting me wet!" Joel said.

Tucker giggled and splashed some more. Then Tucker suddenly stopped. He stood up. "Ro-nee," he said, stretching out his arms toward Joel.

"What?"

"Ro-nee," Tucker repeated.

Joel wrapped a towel around Tucker and lifted him out of the tub.

"Doe Ro-nee," Tucker said, tapping Joel on his bare chest.

Joel laughed. "Oh, now I get it. Me! Joel Maccarone! Doe Ro-nee."

Tucker beamed.

Joel set Tucker on the bathroom rug and rubbed him dry with the towel. "OK, now a pair of pants for the most brilliant kid in the world." Joel pulled the pants onto Tucker.

"Well, well," said a gravelly voice behind him. "Looks like you have everything under control."

Joel turned around. Rachel stood in the doorway, her hands on her hips and a smile on her face. She wore a Scum and the Suds T-shirt. "See, Joel. I told you you'd be great. Check out my Scum and the Suds T-shirt!"

Joel's heart plunged. He looked away from Rachel. He couldn't bear to see Rachel wearing the T-shirt she had promised him! He couldn't believe it. After all he'd gone through.

"Thanks for giving Tucker a bath," Rachel said in a hoarse voice. "And what a smart idea. Taking your shirt off, I mean. He usually has me soaked," Rachel said. "Oh, but you should have heard Scum and the Suds. Awesome. Totally awesome," she croaked. "Thanks so much, Joel. I was worried when I found this." She pulled a pacifier out of her shorts pocket. "Tucker can really be trouble without his opah."

"Opah?"

"That's what he calls his pacifier." Rachel opened up the sack she was holding. "Look, Joel. I got this for you." Her words came out in a raspy whisper. She held up a Scum and the Suds T-shirt. "I yelled so loud they gave me two."

Joel's heart skipped several beats. A Scum and

the Suds T-shirt. She had gotten him one, after all. Wait until he showed Ralphie!

"But listen, Joel. I was wondering if you could help me out with another emergency."

"Another what?"

"Emergency," Rachel repeated.

Amazing. Absolutely amazing. She had said the *E* word twice, and Joel's skin hadn't prickled once.

"Yeah. The last Friday in July, Warm Corpse is going to be at the mall!"

"The last Friday in July?" Joel muttered. He had almost forgotten. "Sorry, I can't. I'll be with the JAs in the Rockies. Mountain biking."

"Don't you have to pass EP first?"

Joel looked at Tucker, all clean and shiny and wearing a new pair of pull-up diapers.

"Piece of cake," Joel said.

"Cake," Tucker repeated, and threw his arms around Joel.

"P.U. Nice job, matey!" Captain squawked from on top of Rachel's head. Well, maybe Joel didn't have *everything* under control.

But what did it matter? He could already feel himself careening down a mountain, fresh air all around him.